# SAUNCEY
## and Mr. King's Gallery

by
**Clara Ann Simmons**

## illustrated by
## Charles Geer

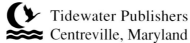 Tidewater Publishers
Centreville, Maryland

Text copyright © 1997 by Clara Ann Simmons
Illustrations copyright © 1997 by Charles Geer
Printed in Hong Kong

Sauncey and her mama lived in Washington City. That is
what young America's capital was called in 1822. They lived
in Mr. Charles Bird King's new house on 12th Street. Mr. King
was a famous artist. He had studied at the Royal Academy in
London, England, for a long time. Then he came back to
America and built his big house just a few blocks from where
President Monroe lived.

The house had skylights and a long gallery. The walls were
covered with portraits he painted.

Mama was Mr. King's cook and Sauncey helped her. What she really wanted to do was be important like the people in the pictures. All the fashionable people came to have their pictures painted by Mr. King. Generals came. Senators came. Elegant ladies came. Sauncey's favorite picture was the beautiful lady in the velvet dress with curls piled on her head.

Sometime Sauncey wanted to meet these visitors.

One day Sauncey was watching Mama stir currant cake
batter. She leaned her elbows on the wooden kitchen table and
rested her head on her hands. Her feet were doing a little dance
and there was a wide smile on her round face. She was hoping
Mama would give her the spoon to lick.

"Stop your fidgeting, here's the spoon," Mama finally said as she poured the batter into the spider to put over the fire. "Soon as you're finished, sweep this floor clean as a whistle." Mama had to go down to Center Market to find a nice canvasback duck for dinner.

Sauncey wished she could go, too. Center Market was where everyone went to get vegetables, fruit, fish, and fowl. It was by Pennsylvania Avenue, the wide street full of muddy ruts that went from the Capitol to the President's House. It was the busiest place in Washington City. There were people every-

where. There were carriages and horses, even some cows and pigs. The botanical garden, theatres, and hotels were on the avenue. The Indian Queen was one of the best hotels. It had sixty rooms.

When Mama left, Sauncey grabbed the broom. Sweeping the floor was hateful, but Mama wouldn't like it if she found one crumb when she got back. Sauncey tried to make it fun by doing a little dance as she swept. She pretended she was a grand lady with a feather in her turban. She would ride around in her carriage and visit people for tea and cakes.

Maybe Mr. King would paint her picture!

A few days later Mama said she was going to the market because Mr. King was having an important visitor for dinner. She told Sauncey to scrub and cut up the turnips. Sauncey dumped a bucket of water in the stone basin. She started jabbing

at the hated turnips. Just then Jed, the yard boy, came clattering
in with a load of kindling for the woodbox.

"Have you heard the news?" he asked.

Sauncey said the only news she knew was turnips.

"Indians is the news," Jed told her. He said they were all over
the place down on Pennsylvania Avenue. They were riding
around in carriages and staying at the Indian Queen Hotel.

Sauncey knew Jed was just trying to scare her, so she said, "All you probably saw was Pocahontas's picture on the Indian Queen's sign." But Jed said cross his heart, the Indians were here. The government brought them to see the city. The government bought them fancy clothes. They had on yellow buckskin shoes, blue pantaloons, and calico shirts. Their clothes were decorated with lace and tassels. Sauncey really didn't want to believe him.

Later on, when Mama was back and frying some oysters, Sauncey asked her if she'd heard about Indians. "Jed's right," Mama said. The government brought delegations of Indians from the Great Plains to make treaties. The government showed them all over the city and gave them presents.

But most important, Mr. King's guest for dinner was Major Thomas L. McKenney. The major wanted Mr. King to paint the

Indians' pictures for his new museum at the War Department. Major McKenney's museum was full of beautiful things the Indians had made. There were capes decorated with porcupine quills and beads, feather headdresses, a big birch bark canoe, and lots of other things. Now the major wanted Mr. King to paint pictures of all the Indians who came to town.

War Department, Indians, blue pantaloons, the Indian Queen
Hotel—Sauncey didn't know what to think, and that night she
dreamed of them all.

The next morning when everyone was out, Sauncey decided to sneak upstairs to the gallery to look at the lady with the curls. Just as she got there, she heard "Knock, knock, knock" on the big front door.

She darted into the hall, opened the door a crack, and stared. There stood one of the tallest men she had ever seen. Half of his face was dyed redder than his skin. Red horsetail hairs stuck up from his head. He looked very stern.

An Indian! Sauncey shoved the door shut.

"Knock, knock, knock" again. She didn't know what to do; maybe she could tell him no one was home. She opened the door a little, and there were two more Indians in buffalo robes standing beside the tall one, and another man.

The other man said he was the interpreter and that the Indians had come to have their pictures painted.

Oh, oh, oh! Pigtails flying in all directions, Sauncey skittered down to the kitchen to get Mama to help. Then she remembered, Mama was at the market. Mr. King was out. Jed was at the town well. She was all alone with these red men and she was very, very scared.

Well, she had wanted to meet visitors. Now she'd better think of something to do. She filled a tray with pieces of currant cake and mugs of new cider. If she kept them busy eating they couldn't do anything else.

She told them Mr. King was out and please sit down.

The tall man said he was Sharitarish.

The man with hoops in his ears said he was Peskelechaco.

The man in the eagle feather headdress said he was Petalesharo. They were from the great Pawnee Nation. The government had brought them to see the sights. They had seen churches, farms, a battleship, and a circus. Now they would have their pictures painted for everyone to see.

When Mr. King got back he found Petalesharo, Sharitarish, Peskelechaco, and the interpreter sitting in a circle on the floor having cake and cider with Sauncey. They were all laughing and talking.

The Pawnee braves were showing her the round silver peace medal that President Monroe had given each of them. It had his picture on the front and on the back it said, "Peace and Friendship."

Mr. King thought Sauncey had been very, very brave.

Later on Mr. King took Sauncey, and Jed too, to see the delegation dance in front of the President's House. It was a very cold day, but still thousands and thousands of people came to watch. Government clerks, lawyers, merchants, sailors, even ladies were there. People bought hot potatoes from a peddler to warm their insides and hands.

The Indians didn't seem to mind the cold one bit. All they had on were red loincloths. They danced for three hours. Their dances told stories about their hunting, war, and tomahawks. Then the delegation went back home to the Great Plains and other ones came.

Chiefs of all the great nations came to see Washington City and have their pictures painted. They had names like Pushmataha, Sequoyah, and Yahahajo. They were Sauk and Fox, Shawnee, Sioux, Creek, Cherokee, Seminole, Choctaw—all the great nations.

Sauncey knew all of them. She often watched Mr. King paint their pictures. She was glad people would be able to go to the museum and look at them.

But what made her gladdest was that one day when she went
to the gallery, there was her very own picture hanging with all

the rest. Mr. King wanted people to notice her; she had entertained the Pawnee Indian chiefs.

# Historical Note

Charles Bird King was born in 1785 in Newport, Rhode Island. When he was fifteen, he was apprenticed to Edward Savage, an artist in New York City. Five years later he sailed to London to study at the Royal Academy with other American artists: Benjamin West, John Trumbull, and Thomas Sully. King remained in England studying for over ten years.

He became a successful portrait painter and in 1819 built a large house in Washington, D.C., where he had his portrait gallery. Distinguished people came to have their portraits done, and King became active in the social life of the city. His work came to the attention of Thomas L. McKenney, Superintendent of Indian Affairs. McKenney had a deep understanding of the Indians' way of life, but knew it was changing. He commissioned King to paint the Indians' portraits for future generations to see. He also began a museum to save their artifacts.

King painted the Indians from 1821 to 1842, portraying at least 143 individuals and receiving over $3,500 in fees. Francis Trollope called them "excellent likenesses, as are all the portraits I have seen from the hands of that gentleman."

In 1837, Major McKenney and a partner published the three-volume *History of the Indian Tribes of North America,* which included many of King's portraits with biographical sketches. It was a great success.

Charles Bird King never married, but he had a great love of children and would invite them to his studio to hear stories and play.

As for Sauncey and her mama, there were over 4,000 free blacks in Washington, D.C., in the 1820s.

Major McKenney's office and museum were placed in the War Department building in 1824. For the story's flow, the collection is put there a few years earlier.